AMAZING RACING CARS

STOCK CARS

BY ASHLEY GISH

CREATIVE EDUCATION • CREATIVE PAPERBACKS

Published by Creative Education and Creative Paperbacks
P.O. Box 227, Mankato, Minnesota 56002
Creative Education and Creative Paperbacks are imprints of
The Creative Company
www.thecreativecompany.us

Design by The Design Lab
Production by Joe Kahnke
Art direction by Rita Marshall
Printed in China

Photographs by Alamy (Cal Sport Media, Jeffrey Isaac Greenberg 5), Dreamstime (Walter Arce), Getty Images (Robert Laberge, RacingOne/ISC Archives), Newscom (LVMS Pool/Icon Sportswire 007, Jeffrey Vest/Icon Sportswire CCR), Shutterstock (Action Sports Photography, Matthew Jacques, Vdant85)

Library of Congress Cataloging-in-Publication Data
Names: Gish, Ashley, author.
Title: Stock cars / Ashley Gish.
Series: Amazing racing cars.
Includes bibliographical references and index.
Summary: A fast-paced, high-interest introduction to stock cars, modified race cars known for their aftermarket parts and use in oval track races. Also included is a biographical story about stock car driver Darrell Wallace Jr.
Identifiers:
ISBN 978-1-64026-292-8 (hardcover)
ISBN 978-1-62832-824-0 (pbk)
ISBN 978-1-64000-422-1 (eBook)
This title has been submitted for CIP processing under LCCN 2019049517.

CCSS: RI.1.1, 2, 4, 5, 6, 7; RI.2.2, 5, 6, 7, 10; RI.3.1, 5, 7, 8; RF.1.1, 3, 4; RF.2.3, 4

First Edition HC 9 8 7 6 5 4 3 2 1
First Edition PBK 9 8 7 6 5 4 3 2 1

Table of Contents

The first stock car races featured normal family cars.

Stock cars look like regular cars. But their **engines** are built for speed. People began racing stock cars in the 1930s. The National Association for Stock Car Auto Racing (NASCAR) formed in 1948.

engines machines that make vehicles move by burning fuel

AUTO SALES & BODY CO.
Martinsville, Va.
21
4
67

MUSTANG
MOOG
Edelbrock
SUNOCO
GOODYEAR

The pit crew repairs and refuels a car in a matter of seconds.

Today, stock cars are built with **aftermarket** parts. Everything from the car's body to its tires is changed to be lighter and stronger.

aftermarket describing parts that are bought to replace existing parts

Seat harnesses and window nets help keep drivers safe.

Sponsor logos cover the cars' bodies. Stock cars do not have headlights. Instead, they have stickers that look like headlights. The doors do not open. Drivers climb in through the window.

sponsor a person or company that pays for a race car

David Gilliland
Holley
NEXTEL
Checkers
DIRECTV
USG
3M
CLEVITE
Commit
Auto Meter
MAC TOOLS
EA SPORTS
DENSO
JEGS
GOODYEAR
GOODYEAR
Gatorback
BELTS
MOOG
CHASSIS PARTS
SUNOCO
OFFICIAL FUEL NASCAR
CLEVITE
ENGINE PARTS
COMP CAMS
Raybestos
The best in brakes
WIX
FILTERS
Edelbrock
GOODYEAR
EAGLE
#24

MONSTER
SIMPSON
PLATINUM

The inside temperature can be more than 100 °F (37.8 °C) during a race.

Stock car drivers make decisions quickly. They zoom past each other at more than 200 miles (322 km) per hour. A metal roll cage keeps the driver safe if the car flips. Drivers wear **fire suits**. These help keep them safe in a crash.

fire suits suits made from a special material that is resistant to catching fire

Stock cars race on circular or oval racetracks. The cars go around the track many times during each race. These laps add up to hundreds of miles.

It takes only one long race to wear out a stock car's engine.

THE STRAT
HOTEL CASINO SKYPOD
THE STRAT
THE STRAT
MONSTER
CAMRY
MUSTANG
GEICO
14
18

DEWALT

Short tracks are less than one mile (1.6 km) long. Intermediate tracks are between one and two miles (1.6–3.2 km) long. Superspeedways are longer than two miles (3.2 km).

The largest racetrack stadiums hold more than 100,000 fans.

18
MONSTER ENERGY
CAMRY
MOOG
MAHLE
18
12
MONSTER ENERGY
PENNZOIL
Ford
12
FUSION

NASCAR vehicles are required to weigh at least 3,400 pounds (1,542 kg).

NASCAR Cup **Series** races happen all over the United States. Drivers earn points for the number of laps they are in the lead. They also gain points based on their place at the finish line.

series a set of races where drivers compete for a championship

Alabama's Talladega Superspeedway is the longest NASCAR racetrack. It is about 2.7 miles (4.3 km) long. The shortest track is Martinsville Speedway in Virginia. The fastest recorded time around this 0.526-mile track (0.8 km) track was 18.7 seconds.

Most races start with about 40 cars, but some might not finish.

THIS IS
INSIGNIA
43
MENARDS
98
Budweiser
5
BOSTITCH
Lite
2
DODGE
14
CAT
CATERPILLAR
31
DUPONT
24
LOWE'S
48

xfinity
xfinity
ENEOS
42
42
CAMARO
MOOG
MAHLE
COMP

Millions of fans attend stock car races or watch them on TV. Tune in to a NASCAR race. Watch these amazing stock cars zoom laps around the track!

Drivers must strengthen their neck muscles to handle the force of high speeds.

Driver Spotlight: Darrell Wallace Jr.

Darrell Wallace

Jr. began racing when he was nine years old. At first, he raced Bandolero cars. They look like miniature stock cars. In 2005, Darrell won 35 of the season's 48 races. He won a Rookie of the Year award 2010. Two years later, Darrell started his NASCAR career. He is one of the most successful African American race car drivers in history. In 2019, he finished fifth in the Monster Energy NASCAR All-Star Race.

sparco
U.S. AIR FORCE
World Wide Technology
Coca-Cola
STP
MACK
GOODYEAR
ALSCO
U.S. AIR FORCE
sparco

Read More

Colins, Luke. *Stock Cars*. North Mankato, Minn.: Black Rabbit Books, 2017.

Fishman, Jon M. *Cool Stock Cars*. Minneapolis: Lerner, 2019.

Howse, Jennifer. *Monster Energy NASCAR Cup*. New York: AV2, 2018.

Websites

Biography: Danica Patrick
https://www.biography.com/athlete/danica-patrick
Learn about Danica Patrick, one of NASCAR's most famous drivers.

DK Find Out: Race Cars for Kids
https://www.dkfindout.com/us/transportation/history-cars/race-cars/
Read more about different kinds of racing cars, and take a quiz.

NASCAR: Acceleration Nation
https://www.accelerationnation.com/
Learn more about NASCAR, and play interactive games.

Note: Every effort has been made to ensure that the websites listed above are suitable for children, that they have educational value, and that they contain no inappropriate material. However, because of the nature of the Internet, it is impossible to guarantee that these sites will remain active indefinitely or that their contents will not be altered.

Index